EARLY BIRD
STORIES

I Am Quicker!
&
Greedy Gull

Early★Reader

First American edition published in 2023 by Lerner Publishing Group, Inc.

An original concept by Katie Dale
Copyright © 2023 Katie Dale

Illustrated by Forrest Burdett

First published by Maverick Arts Publishing Limited

Licensed Edition
I Am Quicker! & Greedy Gull

Lerner Publications Company
An imprint of Lerner Publishing Group, Inc.
241 First Avenue North
Minneapolis, MN 55401 USA

For reading levels and more information, look up this title at www.lernerbooks.com.

Main body text set in Mikado a. Typeface provided by HVD Fonts.

Library of Congress Cataloging-in-Publication Data

Names: Dale, Katie, author. | Burdett, Forrest, illustrator. | Dale, Katie. I am quicker! |
    Dale, Katie. Greedy gull.
Title: I am quicker! ; & Greedy gull / Katie Dale ; illustrated by Forrest Burdett.
Other titles: I am quicker! (Compilation)
Description: First American edition. | Minneapolis : Lerner Publications, 2023. | Series:
    Early bird readers. Red (Early bird stories) | "First published by Maverick Arts
    Publishing Limited." | Audience: Ages 4–8. | Audience: Grades K–1.
Identifiers: LCCN 2022021655 (print) | LCCN 2022021656 (ebook)
    | ISBN 9781728476469 (lib. bdg.) | ISBN 9781728478500 (pbk.) |
    ISBN 9781728482309 (eb pdf)
Subjects: LCSH: Readers (Primary) | LCGFT: Readers (Publications)
Classification: LCC PE1119.2 .D35218 2023 (print) | LCC PE1119.2 (ebook) |
    DDC 428.6/2—dc23/eng/20220518

LC record available at https://lccn.loc.gov/2022021655
LC ebook record available at https://lccn.loc.gov/20220216566

Manufactured in the United States of America
1-52227-50667-6/22/2022

EARLY BIRD
STORIES

I Am Quicker!
&
Greedy Gull

Katie Dale

Illustrated by
Forrest Burdett

Lerner Publications ◆ Minneapolis

The Letter "Q"

Trace the lower and upper case letter with a finger. Sound out the letter.

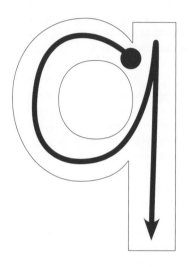

Around,
up,
down,

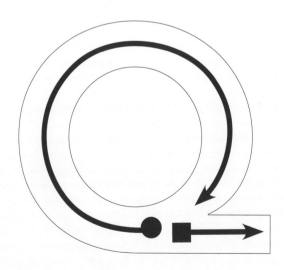

Around,
lift,
cross

Some words to familiarize:

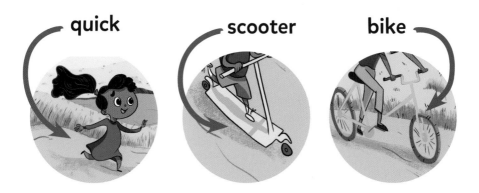

quick

scooter

bike

High-frequency words:

is

Tips for Reading *I Am Quicker!*

- *Practice the words listed above before reading the story.*

- *If the reader struggles with any of the other words, ask them to look for sounds they know in the word. Encourage them to sound out the words and help them read the words if necessary.*

- *After reading the story, ask the reader why Jen was quicker.*

Fun Activity

Think of other ways to travel that are even quicker!

I Am Quicker!

Jen is quick.

Hop, hop, hop!

Tom's scooter is quicker.
Ding, ding, ding!

Mom's bike is quicker.

Ting-a-ling!

Dad's car is quicker.
Honk, honk, honk!

But then . . .

Mom's bike stops.
Ting-a-ling!

Tom's scooter stops.
Ding, ding, ding!

The Letter "G"

Trace the lower and upper case letter with a finger. Sound out the letter.

Around,
up,
down,
around

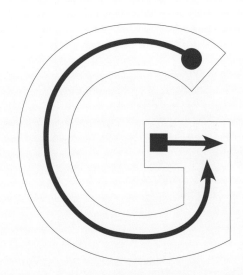

Around,
up,
lift,
cross

Some words to familiarize:

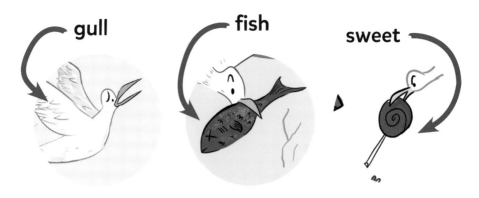

gull

fish

sweet

High-frequency words:

the a

Tips for Reading *Greedy Gull*

- Practice the words listed above before reading the story.

- If the reader struggles with any of the other words, ask them to look for sounds they know in the word. Encourage them to sound out the words and help them read the words if necessary.

- After reading the story, ask the reader why the dog was angry with the gull.

Fun Activity

Think of some other animals that are greedy!

Greedy Gull

The greedy gull gets a nut.
Bad gull!

The greedy gull gets a fish.

The greedy gull gets a sweet.

The greedy gull gets a bun.

Bad gull!

The greedy gull gets a french fry.

The greedy gull gets a roll.
Bad gull!

The greedy gull
gets a hot dog.

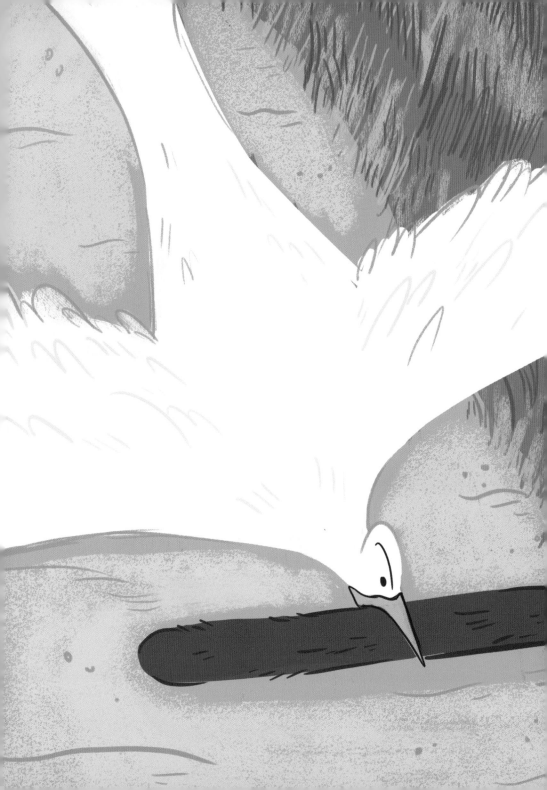

The greedy gull gets a shock!

EARLY BIRD STORIES

COLOR		GRL
Silver	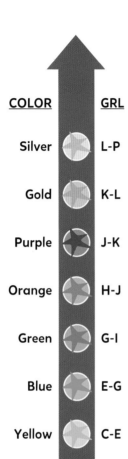	L-P
Gold		K-L
Purple		J-K
Orange		H-J
Green		G-I
Blue		E-G
Yellow		C-E
Red		C-D
Pink		A-C

Leveled for Guided Reading

Early Bird Stories have been edited and leveled by leading educational consultants to correspond with guided reading levels. The levels are assigned by taking into account the content, language style, layout, and phonics used in each book. Visit www.lernerbooks.com for more Early Bird Readers titles!